Sleeping Moon

by DAVID LEWIS ATWELL

Illustrated by DEBBY ATWELL

HOUGHTON MIFFLIN COMPANY

BOSTON   1994

For our children

Library of Congress Cataloging-in-Publication Data

Atwell, David Lewis.

Sleeping moon / by David Lewis Atwell ; illustrated by Debby
Atwell.

p.   cm.

Summary: An orphaned girl feels hope and security when the moon
emerges after Christmas.

ISBN 0-395-68677-6

[1. Moon—Fiction.   2. Orphans—Fiction.   3. Christmas—Fiction.]
I. Atwell, Debby, ill.   II. Title.

PZ7.A893Sl   1994   94-270
[E]—dc20   CIP
                          AC

Printed in the United States of America
BVG   10   9   8   7   6   5   4   3   2   1

Sleeping Moon

Cora arrived at the orphanage before Christmas.

There was nowhere else for her to go.

The children there were all eager to greet her. But Cora
scarcely noticed.

Her mind was elsewhere. Her mind was on the moon.

She could remember the time she'd gazed at the moon, snuggling cozily between her father and mother on the porch swing.

"There's the brightest of night's lights," Mother had said.
"It's the place where all lost things go."
She'd felt so happy then. So safe.

She believed the moon would always be there waiting, full and bright. Now, when she looked from her window, it was as if nothing had changed; nothing had been lost.

Cora did have her own bed and a little bureau for her things. She liked Hiram, the lighthouse keeper, who often ate supper with them and told stories of storms and lost ships.

He promised to let Cora look through one of his
telescopes. They could make the moon look as if it were
so close you could reach out and touch it.

As Christmas drew nearer, Cora felt that something was wrong. Slowly but surely, night after night, the moon was getting smaller.

What if the moon went away? What would happen to
all the lost things? Cora was sure that the moon too
would abandon her.

By Christmas Eve, the moon was nowhere to be found.
Cora ran from window to window, desperately searching the sky.
She must get Hiram, she thought.

The path to the lighthouse began at the edge of the woods.
Cora thought they looked like the biggest woods she had ever
seen. They were certainly the darkest.

A cold wind blew through the trees around her, and the newly fallen snow made the path hard to follow. Her legs ached from the heavy snow, and she felt cold and tired.

Exhausted, she sat down, her eyes on the sky. Through the branches she could see only stars. The moon was gone. Cora shivered and closed her eyes.

Hiram hurried down the path. He looked forward to Christmas
Eve at the orphanage. But when he came to the fresh little
footprints crossing his way, he stopped.

He knelt in the snow, listening intently for a sound.
He stared deeply into the surrounding trees for a sign.
Hiram waited.

Then he saw what looked like a tiny patch of moonlight
at the foot of a great maple tree. *That's strange,* he
thought, looking into the moonless sky. As he moved toward
the light, he heard a small voice.

"It's gone," Cora cried in her sleep. "The moon's gone."
Hiram gently lifted her into his arms and carried her back
to the orphanage.

Cora awoke in her own bed. She thought it was enough just
to be warm again. That was all the Christmas gift she
expected on this morning.

But to Cora's surprise, a long, narrow box awaited her beneath the Christmas tree. Inside it she found a shiny red telescope with a note that read: "Don't give up. Keep looking!"

Night after night Cora searched the sky, peering among the stars. On the third night, she found the smallest sliver of light against the darkened sky.

The moon hadn't gone anywhere, she thought. It had been
there all the time. It was only sleeping!

From that night on, Cora invited the other children to look
through her telescope as the moon grew bright and full.

As they watched, Cora told them how the moon was the place where all lost things go.

Then, as the nights passed, the moon became smaller and smaller. Cora bravely told them everything would be all right.

The children listened. Cora told them the moon was only
sleeping and would awaken again.

And when the moon rose full, it warmed the very heavens with
its brilliance. Nearly as full and bright as the moon
itself were the hopeful faces of Cora and her new friends.
She knew she would never feel completely alone again.